Christmas

Charles M. Schulz

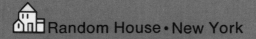
Random House • New York

Lyrics of "O Christmas Tree!" adapted from the TRAPP-FAMILY BOOK OF CHRISTMAS SONGS, selected and arranged by Franz Wasner. Copyright 1950 by Pantheon Books, a Division of Random House, Inc. Reprinted by permission of Pantheon Books, a Division of Random House, Inc.

Library of Congress Cataloging in Publication Data

Schulz, Charles M. A Charlie Brown Christmas. SUMMARY: Charlie Brown undertakes a search for the true meaning of Christmas. [1. Christmas Stories. 2. Cartoons and comics] I. Title.
PN6728.P4S24   1977   741.5′973 [E]   76-57940   ISBN: 0-394-83454-2
ISBN: 0-394-93454-7 lib. bdg.

Manufactured in the United States of America   1 2 3 4 5 6 7 8 9 0

I think there must be something wrong with me, Linus. Christmas is coming, but I'm not happy.

I like getting presents and sending Christmas cards and all that. But I'm still not happy. I always end up feeling depressed.

Charlie Brown, you're the only person I know who can take a wonderful season like Christmas and turn it into a problem. Maybe Lucy's right. Of all the Charlie Browns in the world, you're the Charlie Browniest!

Helloooo in there!

Thanks for the Christmas card you sent me, Violet.

I didn't send you a Christmas card, Charlie Brown.

Don't you know sarcasm when you hear it?

Try to catch snowflakes on your tongue. It's fun.

Rats! Nobody sent me a Christmas card today. I almost wish there weren't a holiday season. I know nobody likes me. Why do we have to have have a holiday season to emphasize it?

Pig-Pen, you're the only person I know who can raise a cloud of dust in a snowstorm.

It's far too early. I never eat December snowflakes. I always wait until January.

They sure look ripe to me.

I think you have
a customer.

May I help you?

I'm in sad shape.

Wait a minute. Before you
begin I must ask that you pay
in advance. Five cents, please.

All right now, what seems to be your trouble?

I feel depressed. I know I should be happy, but I'm not.

Let's pinpoint your fears. Are you afraid of responsibility? You may have hypengyophobia.

I don't think that's quite it.

If you are afraid of cats, you have ailurophasia. If you are afraid of staircases, you have climacaphobia.

Or maybe you have pantophobia. That's the fear of everything.

THAT'S IT!!

Actually, Lucy, my trouble is Christmas. I just don't understand it. Instead of feeling happy, I feel sort of let down.

You need involvement. You need to get involved in some real Christmas project. How would you like to be the director of our Christmas play?

Me? You want *me* to be the director of the Christmas play?

But I don't know anything about directing a Christmas play!

Don't worry! I'll be there to help you. I'll meet you at the auditorium at three o'clock.

Incidentally, I know how you feel about all this Christmas business, getting depressed and all that. It happens to me every year.

I never get what I really want. I always get a lot of stupid toys, or a bicycle, or clothes, or something like that.

What is it you want?

Real estate!

What's going on here? What's this?

"Find the true meaning of Christmas. Win money, money, money! Enter the Christmas Lights and Display Contest."

My own dog, gone commercial! I can't stand it!

I've been looking for you, big brother. Will you please write a letter to Santa Claus for me? You write it, and I'll tell you what I want you to say.

Dear Santa Claus, how have you been? Did you have a nice summer? How is your wife?

I have been extra good this year. So I have a long list of presents that I want.

Please note the size and color of the items, and send as many as possible. If it seems too complicated, make it easy on yourself. Send money. How about tens and twenties?

AUGH!!

EVEN MY BABY SISTER!

TENS AND TWENTIES!!!

This is the music I have selected for the Christmas play.

What kind of Christmas music is that?

Beethoven Christmas music.

What has Beethoven got to do with Christmas? Everyone talks about how great Beethoven was. Beethoven wasn't so great.

What do you mean, Beethoven
wasn't so great?

He never got his picture on bubble gum cards, did he?
Have you ever seen his picture on a bubble gum card?
Huh? How can you say someone is great who's never
had his picture on bubble gum cards!

GOOD GRIEF!

All right! Quiet everybody. Our director will be here any minute, and we'll start rehearsal.

Director? What director?

Charlie Brown.

Oh, no! We're doomed.

This will be the worst Christmas play ever.

Here he comes! Attention everyone.

Here is our director!

Man's best friend!

Well, it's real good seeing you all here. As you know, we are going to put on the Christmas play. One of the first things to insure a good performance is strict attention to the director. I'll keep my directions simple.

If I point to the right, it means focus attention stage right. If I make a slashing motion across my throat, it means cut the scene short. If I spread my hands apart, it means slow down.

It's the spirit of the actors that counts—the interest that they show in their director. Am I right? I said, "Am I right?" Why doesn't anyone answer me?!!

All right now, Lucy, get those costumes and scripts and pass 'em out.

Now the script girl will be handing out your parts.

Frieda, you're the innkeeper's wife.

Do inkeepers' wives have naturally curly hair?

Pig-Pen, you're the innkeeper.

In spite of my outward appearance, I shall try to run a neat inn.

Shermy, you're a shepherd.

Every Christmas it's the same. I always end up playing a shepherd.

BAAAAAAAAA

Snoopy, you'll have to be all the animals in our play.

ROOAAR

All right, all right, Snoopy. Let's get on with this play!

Here, Linus, memorize these lines.

This is ridiculous! I can't memorize something like this so quickly. Why should I be put through such agony? Give me one good reason why I should memorize this!

I'll give you five good reasons.

1–2–3–4–5!

Those are good reasons.

Christmas is not only getting too commercial, it's getting too dangerous.

And get rid of that stupid blanket!!!! What's a Christmas shepherd going to look like holding a stupid blanket like that?

Well this is one Christmas shepherd who's going to keep his trusty blanket with him.

You wouldn't hit an innocent shepherd, would you?

All right, let's rehearse the scene at the inn.

I can't go on. There's too much dust. It's taking the curl out of my naturally curly hair!

Don't think of it as dust. Think of it as the soil of some past great civilization. He may be carrying the soil of ancient Babylon!

Sort of makes you want to treat me with more respect, doesn't it?

You're an absolute mess! Just look at yourself!

On the contrary, I didn't think I looked *that* good.

Sally, come here.

What do you want her for?

She's gonna be your wife.

Isn't he the cutest thing!

He has the nicest sense of humor.

What's the matter, Charlie Brown?

No one around here has the right spirit.

Look, Charlie, let's face it. We all know that Christmas is a big commercial racket. It's run by a big Eastern syndicate, you know.

Well this is one play that's not gonna be commercial. We need the proper mood. We need a Christmas tree.

Hey, perhaps a tree, a great big shiny aluminum Christmas tree. That's it, Charlie Brown! You get the tree. I'll handle this crowd.

Okay, I'll take Linus with me. The rest of you practice your lines.

Get the biggest aluminum tree you can find, Charlie Brown—maybe painted pink! Do something right for a change.

Gee, I didn't know they still made wooden Christmas trees!

This little green one here seems to need a home.

I don't know, Charlie Brown. Remember what Lucy said? This doesn't seem to fit the modern spirit.

I don't care. We'll decorate it, and it'll be just right for our play.

Besides, I think it needs me.

We're back.

Boy are you stupid, Charlie Brown!

What kind of a tree is that? You were supposed to get a *good* tree.

I told you he'd goof it up.

He's not the kind you can depend on to do anything!

You're hopeless, Charlie Brown, completely hopeless.

I guess you were right, Linus. I shouldn't have picked this little tree. I guess I really don't know what Christmas is all about. Isn't there anyone who knows what Christmas is all about????

Sure, Charlie Brown, I can tell you what Christmas is all about.

And there were in the same country shepherds
abiding in the field, keeping watch over their flock
by night.

And, lo, the angel of the Lord came upon them,
and the glory of the Lord shone round about them;
and they were sore afraid.

And the angel said unto them, Fear not: for,
behold, I bring you good tidings of great joy, which
shall be to all people.

For unto you is born this day in the city of
David a Saviour, which is Christ the Lord.

And this shall be a sign unto you; Ye shall find
the babe wrapped in swaddling clothes lying in
a manger.

And suddenly there was with the angel a
multitude of the heavenly host praising God, and
saying,

Glory to God in the highest, and on earth peace,
good will toward men.

And that's what Christmas is all about, Charlie Brown.

Linus is right. I won't let all this commercialism ruin my Christmas. I'll take this little tree home and decorate it. I'll show them it really *will* work in our play.

First prize?!

Oh, well, this commercial dog is not going to ruin my Christmas.

Augh! I've killed it! Everything I touch gets ruined!!

It's not a bad little tree, really.

Maybe it just needs
a little love.

What are they doing with Snoopy's decorations?

You'll see.

Charlie Brown is a blockhead, but he did get a nice tree.

MERRY CHRISTMAS

What's going on here?

CHARLIE BROWN!

Hark! the herald angels sing,
"Glory to the new-born King!
Peace on earth, and mercy mild;
God and sinners reconcil'd!"
Joyful, all ye nations, rise,
Join the triumph of the skies;
With th'angelic hosts proclaim,
"Christ is born in Bethlehem!"
Hark! the herald angels sing,
"Glory to the new-born King!"

Christ, by highest heav'n ador'd,
Christ, the everlasting Lord;
Long desir'd, behold Him come,
Finding here His humble home.
Veil'd in flesh the Godhead see,
Hail th'incarnate Deity!
Pleas'd as man with men to dwell,
Jesus, our Emmanuel!
Hark! the herald angels sing,
"Glory to the new-born King!"

Mild, He lays His glory by,
Born that man no more may die;
Born to raise the sons of earth,
Born to give them second birth.
Ris'n with healing in His wings,
Light and life to all He brings,
Hail, the Son of Righteousness!
Hail, the heav'n born Prince of Peace!
Hark! the herald angels sing,
"Glory to the new-born King!"

Hark! the Herald Angels Sing

Poem by Charles Wesley   Music by Felix Mendelssohn